PUT ON YOUR GLOVES

The Five Battles
Every Christian Must Win

Dr. John Polis

Put On Your Gloves: The Five Battles Every Christian Must Win

ISBN: 978-0-9898310-3-1

©2015 John Polis

John Polis Ministries, 600 The Drive, Fairmont, WV 26554
www.johnpolis.com

ENDORSEMENTS

God's leaders are under attack to 'take them out' if possible. John Polis has heard from God concerning timely reminders that every leader needs to hear. This book will challenge your spirit and ignite a flame in your commitment. I encourage you to share this book with every leader you know.

Apostle Naomi Dowdy
Republic of Singapore

I recommend Apostle John Polis's latest book as a necessary manual for all active duty warriors in the Lord's Army! Polis is a true warrior in the spiritual and the natural, in both the heavenly and earthly realms, who is highly qualified to give practical knowledge and wisdom - because he has lived it. Born and raised in the tough, scrappy towns of Western Pennsylvania, trained in the US Marine Corps, plus decades of ministry and family life experiences prepared him for crucial assignments on many fronts. Now he shares how to win the five primary battles that every Christian faces. This book is essential for anyone in ministry and every Christian who wants to fulfill Christ's will – to be a winner and receive a "well done good and faithful servant." Your assignment will always include battles – it's imperative that you know the enemy and understand the obstacles and learn how to fight effectively to WIN!

Dr. John P. Kelly
International Convening Apostle
International Coalition of Apostolic Leaders

In a day of compromise and cowardice, generals of the faith are bringing a strong, sobering and scriptural word for courageous Christians. Dr. John Polis, a US Marine, has emerged as a leader at the front lines and brilliantly outlines a winning strategy for winning five major battles every Christian must wage to experience total victory in their lives and future of their families. This is a must-read for those who want to thrive in challenging times.

Robert J. Hrabak, Jr.
Lieutenant Colonel, USAF (ret)

"The apostle's place is to make you - the champion of God - ready to fight in any battle for which you are called up to engage the enemy, fully prepared and with fire and passion, knowing not only that God is on your side, but also the steady hand of the apostle." This book will prepare every Christian to win the battles for truth, our families,

our souls, our faith, and our ministries. Apostle Dr. John Polis, as a spiritual father but also as a general, gives strategies in every one of these battle arenas to come out victorious. After reading this book, one realizes that we must never abandon our post or our position. This is a 'must-read' for such a time as this. I highly recommend it.

Pastor Kris Walls
New Life Church, Seward, PA

We are in a constant battle for our hearts and minds in every aspect of our daily life. We see in these five battles what the devices of the devil are for taking our light from us so that he may sow more darkness. In facing these battles we must know we have been equipped to win every fight. I highly recommend this book as a fresh and current word for the Church in an hour when society is trying to push us out of the marketplace into a corner declaring the Church and God's word are obsolete and out of touch with today's society. May God show you His truth and His plan for victory in these five areas of your life.

Mike Cutright
Chaplain, Tygart Valley Regional Jail

TABLE OF CONTENTS

FOREWORD

Participating in the publishing of Dr. John Polis' books has always been an adventure in revelation. This latest offering is no exception - much of what follows I would have to liken to what the apostle Paul referred to as 'strong meat' (Hebrews 5:12-14), and is not for the faint of heart. Vital (life-giving) revelation is that way, intended to slice and insert itself into our way of seeing things (naturally) so that we can see them the way God sees them (supernaturally).

The general intent of a foreword such as this is to introduce you to the work that follows. Allow me instead to introduce you to the man, in a sense, as in truth it is the integrity of character which has the more lasting impact than any body of work. Being able to call Dr. John my spiritual father is an honor that I do not esteem lightly, and his example of servant-leadership and the true love of a father have forever marked my existence. By simply being consistent in obeying the voice of God, his influence has expanded worldwide, and literally thousands of souls have been impacted by the apostolic dynamic at work in his life.

Having witnessed Dr. John fight and win spiritual battles for three decades now, I have to say that you are in the best of hands as you allow this General of the faith to train you for war. Augmenting his spiritual combat experience is the constant flow of revelation that comes only from spending time with the Commander-in-Chief, Jesus Christ Himself, in order to ascertain and develop the strategies to fight and win these five battles that all Christians will face, sooner or later. I entreat you to prepare your heart to receive this life-changing revelation of spiritual authority from one who has lived it.

Tony Ebert
Psalmist
June 2015

Chapter 1

LEADERSHIP IN A LETTER

"Paul, an apostle of Jesus Christ by the commandment of God our Saviour, and the Lord Jesus Christ, our hope; to Timothy, a true son in the faith: Grace, mercy, and peace, from God our Father and Jesus Christ our Lord." (1 Timothy 1:1 NKJV)

The apostle Paul was a fascinating man. I could write several books on his passion and revelatory nature, but I won't because that would not fulfill my goal with this book. However, Paul is where we need to start in order to set the ground work, with his letter to his protégé, his spiritual son, Timothy.

When we talk about the battles that men and women in the Body of Christ as a whole have to face, it is imperative that we start from a beginning and then work our way into understanding what it is that we must be prepared for in the future.

I know you are thinking that I am going to start in Genesis 1:1, but for the direction of this title 1 Timothy 1:1 will provide our foundation with an example of faith, leadership, and fight, because an understanding of each of them will arm us with the tools we need to win each of the battles that we must face.

When Paul wrote this letter to Timothy, this young pastor was facing some heavy opposition. Ephesus is experiencing great challenges. False doctrines are sweeping the land, public worship is being threatened, and a lack of mature leadership was taking its toll. Sounds like the time we are living in right now, doesn't it?

Paul knew that Timothy needed to be prepared for the battles that were ahead of him. He understood that, as an apostle, it was his duty to see to it that Timothy had the spiritual playbook that would not only sustain him, but also the message of Christ that was gaining in significance in the region. Who better to help Timothy adjust his breastplate? There was no one as qualified as his spiritual father, Paul.

After all, by this time, he had been stoned, jailed, and beaten more than his fair share, and now his focus had to be about training Timothy for the battles that were to lie ahead of him. *"Paul, an apostle of Jesus Christ..."* was about to hold his first infantry training with a pen and a couple sheets of parchment.

"But God chose the foolish things of the world to shame the wise; God chose the weak things of the world to shame the strong." (1 Corinthians 1:27 NIV)

How can a letter train a battalion?

The anointing, that's how. Paul was tremendous at writing his discourse in letter form. It was probably because it was his only real mode of communication when he found himself locked up in prison cells. It really doesn't matter how he acquired the skill, the reality is that he did and we are better for it, even today.

Knowing your position and using what you have at your disposal is first base when it comes to fighting these battles. Paul was demonstrating to Timothy, and to us, that we must not focus on the fact that everything is not perfect, but instead on the truth that we have more than we need to effectively stand our post and engage the enemy in the battles that are before us.

Paul was locked in jail for spreading the Word of Jesus Christ and making disciples of men. That was his rank and order in the battle for the Kingdom of God. Paul discovered his position in the fight and used every weapon available to him to carry out his purpose (part of the fight) here on earth.

He engaged his enemy and dominated him to the point that the New Testament has as much his stamp on it as it does Jesus, the One which the whole Bible is centered around.

Paul was a leader. He led. He led by example. He led by the Spirit of God. But no matter what, he led. He never abandoned his post. Maybe his weapon of choice would change from time to time, but Paul was a leader, an apostle of Jesus Christ. He was always ready to pick up a weapon and stand a post. In the end, every battle plan must be carried out under the tutelage of a leader.

In this case, Jesus enlisted Paul and called him up for duty three days later. Why? Because Jesus knew his leadership skills would be just what a boy named Timothy needed as he was being prepared to man the watch. Again, Paul was the perfect choice. Why? Because leaders lead, whether by letter or lecture - they take their place in the front of the room seriously and that is what you and I must do, when it comes to submitting to the leader that God has placed in your life. Allow God to reveal where your post in these battles is and then take your place.

Chapter 2

AN APOSTLE'S PLACE

"Paul, an apostle (a special messenger) of Christ Jesus by appointment and command of God our Savior and of Christ Jesus (the Messiah), our Hope..." (1 Timothy 1:1 AMP)

As an apostle, I am fascinated by the revelations that God has given me on this important office. It's an unbelievable honor to serve God in this capacity, but I am never without the reminder that this placement in the Kingdom of God is an appointment and a command.

Part of the role of an apostle is to prepare God's troops for battle, a crucial assignment on many fronts. As we can see in this verse, the chief apostle Paul demonstrated this very point: that apostles are in many respects teachers with a mandate to guide men and women of God in the strategies of battle on the earth.

"For we wrestle not against flesh and blood, but against principalities, against powers, against the rulers of the darkness of this world, against spiritual wickedness in high places." (Ephesians 6:12)

Many believe that there is no reason to be prepared for battles because they don't believe that a battle is going on in the first place. Nothing, and I mean nothing, could be further from the truth.

"For we are not wrestling with flesh and blood [contending only with physical opponents], but against the despotisms, against the powers, against [the master spirits who are] the world rulers of this present darkness, against the spirit forces of wickedness in the heavenly (supernatural) sphere." (Ephesians 6:12 AMP)

Paul demonstrates the urgency of preparedness as he talks to his true son, Timothy, through pen and paper, preparing his heart and mind for the battles that would lay ahead of him.

"Paul, an apostle of Jesus Christ...to Timothy, a true son in the faith..."

Whenever I read this passage there is something so subtle that pulls at my spirit. *"...Timothy, a true son in the faith..."* Paul could have just written, *"Timothy, a son in the faith..."* and I don't believe it was by accident or an overzealous translator that place that word 'true' in the context of this scripture.

true *(adjective)*: in accordance with fact or reality, loyal or faithful, honest, real, genuine, authentic; consistent.

What powerful adjectives to describe a person, any person for that matter. But to have your leader see you in such high regard is worth noting. Timothy's name means "honored by God." How Timothy must have felt when Paul's salutation affirmed his character and integrity with a four letter word.

It is a mistake not to take things like faithfulness, honesty, and consistency seriously. In every one of these battles, you and I will have the opportunity to abandon our character, especially when the battle is at its most intense. And believe me, when you do so, defeat is inevitable, because part of the fight is staying true to the faith in the midst of it.

Timothy had every reason in the world to retreat from his post and abandon his character. Paul, his leader, was locked away in prison. The church at Ephesus was being bombarded by false teachers and doctrines, while public displays of worship were also being challenged.

I believe Timothy could have used a reprieve from all the issues surrounding the fight for the faith. But God did the greater - He sent a letter from the hands of his leader. And at that moment, I believe he needed two things, and Paul was both - a father and a general.

An apostle is inherently two things: (1) a father and (2) a general.

"Paul, an apostle of Jesus Christ..."

As I stated before, the mandate of apostles is of great importance and great responsibility. But our role is not a straightforward one either; it holds multiple functions under one umbrella, so to speak.

Fatherhood

Apostles are also spiritual fathers. Paul's focus in this text is a position of love and tenderness. As a father, I can tell you that as I operate in the office of an apostle, my children are the best part of me. When I see them, my heart melts because of the love and care that I have for them. Of course there are times when I've had to be stern with them as I was training them for the things that they would have to encounter in life. But every part of my interaction with them has been rooted in my love for them. The same is true for my spiritual sons and daughters. Yes, I have to train, but I must also love. The office of apostleship only works when the two are present in a Godly balance, because training turns to cruelty if love is not present to balance it. My love for God and my love for them must be the nucleus of any training exercise and combat maneuver, and that is what Timothy desperately needed when Paul's letter arrived that day.

Yes, Paul was under a heavy mandate delivered on the dusty road of Damascus by his Commander-in-Chief, Jesus, but no matter how heavy his own burden, Paul could not neglect his responsibility to Timothy as his father in the faith.

"...to my true son, Timothy..."

I am sure that there were other men around Paul, claiming to be his son in the faith. We have all had people around us at one time or another, pronouncing their undying commitment to us, only to reveal at some point that their intentions were not of devotion. But Timothy was special to God and the advancement of the Gospel in the region.

As an apostle, Paul was not only responsible for getting Timothy ready for battle, he also had the task of loving him through the process. He had to function with a balanced wisdom, teaching discipline in the Word and fellowship in the faith.

The responsibility and role of spiritual fathers seems lost in our society. Some have abused the rank to such a point that people refuse to follow the leadership that apostles bring. But every aspect of that must change in order for the apostles to effectively ready the troops for the battles to come.

The General

Getting God's people ready for the battles that are ahead can be a daunting task if you look at it from the surface. The generalship of apostles is under its own attack. As generals, commanders in God's army, we teach and train soldiers in spiritual matters, much like generals and commanders do in natural military situations.

As a United States Marine, I understand the context and importance of being prepared for battle from a personal perspective.   I know what it means to strategize for war and to develop battle plans. I also understand rank and order in combat preparedness and engagement situations, which is why I can tell you that the rank of general is one of crucial placement.

For instance, a general in the United States military is responsible for the combat readiness of its troops. In addition, the general handles the training and supervision of the United States National guard during peace time.

Spiritually, Paul was doing the same. He was taking Timothy through combat readiness by imploring him with the Word of God. He was taking the opportunity to supervise Timothy's training one-on-one while locked in a prison cell.

He was taking advantage of the time he was confined, using it to teach, instruct and supervise Timothy. He was saying in essence, "I am responsible for getting you ready for these battles that you have ahead of you, Timothy." Paul understood the responsibility of his rank as an apostle in God's army. And as such, he knew that he had to prepare those in active service of the kingdom of God to fight against God's enemies in the earth.

Here we have the foundation of success in God's army: an apostle clearly fighting to prepare an army of believers that would follow in his footsteps. And included in that was all the tender love and affection of a proud father, looking at the development and maturity of his son, Timothy.

There is no readiness for war without the readiness of an apostle. Knowing that an apostle has a place in the training of your spiritual readiness to fight is as important as which weapons to use at what time and in what maneuver.

The apostle's place is to make you - the champion of God - ready to fight in any battle for which you are called up to engage the enemy, fully prepared and with fire and passion, knowing not only that God is on your side, but also the steady hand of His apostle.

Chapter 3

PUSH BACK

"And from the days of John the Baptist until now the kingdom of heaven suffers violence and the violent take it by force." (Matthew 11:12 NKJV)

When Jesus mentions John the Baptist in this verse, it was not by accident or coincidence. The murder of John the Baptist would be chronicled as the first violent act against a believer in Jesus Christ.

John was as the Bible says, the messenger, a forerunner of the message of the kingdom of God in the earth, and he would also be the first of many brethren who would suffer for Christ's sake.

The word 'suffer' in the Greek means *to crowd oneself into; to press into*. Some verses translate it as to mean *experiences* or *the experience of* - which means that the kingdom of God experiences a crowding or pressing into it on a daily basis. *"Since the days of John the Baptist until now,"* or up to this time, the kingdom of darkness has been on the warpath pressing itself into the earth forcefully and relentlessly.

Have you ever been in a situation where there was pushing and shoving going on? Maybe you've witnessed the madness that happens at a store or concert when people are all trying to squeeze in a small doorway at the same time. If you have, then you know what it feels like to have someone pressing past you to get where they want to go. The same thing is happening in the earth today.

Darkness is on a two-fold mission to crowd in as much darkness into the earth as it can, until its time expires for good. It also aims to press against those who believe in Jesus Christ to the point of surrender. But there's another side to that suffering: the way that we, believers in Jesus Christ, respond to that pressing.

"From the time of John the Baptist until now, violent people have been trying to take over the kingdom of heaven by force." (Matthew 11:12 CEV)

But you and I have to make up in our minds that like John the Baptist that we will not surrender and that we will never quit. We will NEVER give up!

John the Baptist taught us early on what *"for Christ I live and for Christ I die"* means (Philippians 1:21). But it's more than lip service that is needed today. It's more than standing with your battle armor on only to protect yourself against the attack of the enemy. Again, there is another side to this whole warfare. On that side, we become the opposition to the kingdom of darkness.

We are to be forceful people. We should be doing the pressing against, the crowding out. The kingdom of darkness should be feeling the pushing (pressing) of the Church on its back. Spiritual wickedness (satan and his demonic regime) should be pushed from the earth, not us (the followers of Christ Jesus). We should have the attitude, "Who do you think we are?"

God Almighty created the earth for us. It is our gift from our Father - you have no business tearing up or tearing down anything that God gave to His people. Darkness should feel the pressure from the people of God. All of hell should feel the force of our strength pushing against it, in unity and in one accord.

How many of you know someone who is just physically violent? Are they ready to 'throw down' at the drop of a hat? They want to fight, if you look at them the wrong way. If you know someone like that, then you know the volatility that comes along with their personality. You know how on guard you have to be when dealing with a person that is of a violent nature.

We need to be spiritually violent. We need to be ready to throw down at the drop of a hat in the battles that God needs us to fight in. As believers, we are to be of a violent nature spiritually. The spiritually violent people take the kingdom of God forcefully.

"...the violent take it by force."

Though the message of the Cross is wrapped firm in the love of God and His compassion for mankind, there is a time to be forceful in the message of the kingdom of Heaven. We must push back with all the strength and power available to us, because as spiritual warriors, you and I are charged with winning the battles that are vital to the future of the world as we know it.

We have no room for those who won't engage the enemy, because he is challenging us to a fight every time he sees the opportunity. Don't shy away from these battles, because they are already won. God is for you, and He is more than the whole world against you (Romans 8:31).

Chapter 4

THE BATTLE FOR TRUTH

"But if our gospel [good news] be hid, it is hid to them are lost [perishing]. In whom the god of this world hath blinded the minds of them which believe not, lest the light of the glorious gospel of Christ, who is the image of God, should shine unto them." (2 Corinthians 4:3-4)

Right now as you read this book, there is a war raging over the Truth. What is truth, and where does it reside? Truth resides on a higher realm; the realm of the Spirit. You and I carry the Truth, (the Word of God) to the world at large.

"So Jesus was saying to those Jews who had believed Him, "If you continue in My word, then you are truly disciples of Mine; Then you will know the truth, and the truth will set you free." (John 8:31-32 NIV). And so the battle begins...

The adversary is doing everything that he can to keep people blinded to the truth that is right before their eyes.

When a person is physically blind and in constant darkness, you could put a flashlight right in their face but they cannot see the light. That is the same with people who reject the Gospel: the truth and light of Jesus can be shining brightly, right before their eyes (2 Corinthians 4:6), but still they will not see it. That's because satan - the god of this world - has blinded them to the Truth. His mission is to keep as many people as he can blinded to the truth of Jesus for as long as he can.

How does satan blind people's minds from seeing the glorious light of the gospel that shines in the face of Jesus? How does satan blind their minds? He blinds their minds with lies and deception. I like to say it this way: 'Jesus is hiding in plain sight.' He is not hiding himself, but He is being hidden to those who give heed to everything else but Him.

"But if our gospel be hid, it is hid to them that are lost." (2 Corinthians 4:3-4)

The Bible says in 1 Timothy 4:1 (NKJV), "*Now the Spirit speaks expressly, that in latter times some will depart from the faith, giving heed to seducing spirits and doctrines of devils.*"

Even some of the faithful will be drawn away by seducing spirits and doctrines of devils, so think about how strong the pull by those forces is on those who don't know Jesus at all. The devil has a storehouse of lies that he pulls from in order to deceive and manipulate people, and yes, sometimes even the very elect (Matthew 24:24) will fall prey to his tactics; which is why we must stand fast in the faith. Taking a position of passivity where the truth of God's Word is concerned is what I believe will leave many prey to the deceit of the enemy.

Some of these lies actually lie in the 'isms' of world religions: Islam, Shintoism, Confucionism, the list goes on and on. The cults, Jehovah's Witness, Mormonism, and many other world religions, are all "doctrines of devils."

As the *"father of lies"* (John 8:44), satan uses these lies to blind the minds of people so they cannot see the truth that comes to us through Jesus. The truth is that Jesus is the way, the truth and the life. No man comes to the Father, but by Him. (Read John 14:6.)

Either Jesus was telling the truth or Jesus was a liar. But we know that He was the truth in bodily form, and there is no in-between. There are no shortcuts to truth. I know that we are being conditioned to take the shortcuts instead of the scenic route, but we must be careful not to adopt a secular mindset when it comes to the things of God.

Well, what do we do? How do we combat these lies? We use our weapons to fight!

"For though we walk in the flesh, we do not war after the flesh, (for the weapons of our warfare are not carnal, but mighty through God to the pulling down of strong holds); casting down imaginations, and every high thing that exalts itself against the knowledge (or the truth) of God, and bringing into captivity every thought to the obedience of Christ." (2 Corinthians 10:3-5 NKJV)

What are our mighty weapons? It's the Bible... It's the B-I-B-L-E...it's the Word of God. It's the anointing of the Holy Ghost, the name of and the blood of Jesus. Those weapons are enough to defeat any lie, deceit, stronghold, bondage or sickness. Those lies that have blinded the minds of people are no match for the weapons that Jesus secured for us. We can give the truth to those who are blinded and they will see the light and understand the truth of the Word of God. There is hope in this fight.

Yes, millions, even billions of people are being deceived, and that battle is right in our backyard. But you and I are going to win the battle for truth in four distinct areas:

1. We must know the truth. *"Then said Jesus to those Jews which believed on him, If you continue in my word, then are ye my disciples indeed. And ye shall know the truth, and the truth shall make you free."* (John 8:31-32)

We must have an experiential knowledge of the truth; not just an intellectual knowledge, but a revelational knowledge of the truth in your heart. This can't be truth that only gives mental assent to what is read; it has to be truth that is rooted in your experience and faith in a truth that is beyond your comprehension. This truth is embedded in your heart and it provokes you to action.

You shall know the truth and the truth shall produce a result in your life. You shall know the truth and the truth shall set you free, because once you truly know something, you can't be bound by what is not truth. Once you know that Jesus is a healer, you can't be bound by sickness.

For whatever is true about your healing, that will bring healing to you. Whatever is true about your money, that will bring finances to you. Whatever is true about any bondage in your life or addiction according to the Word of God, when you know that truth by revelation, it'll free you from it.

*"You shall **know** the **truth** and the **truth will make** you free."*

But we must first know it. But we won't know it unless we do what Jesus said: "*You must continue in my Word*" (John 8:31). Continue to learn it. Continue to meditate on it. Continue to hear it from the Holy Spirit and through your five-fold ministry leaders. Listen to your apostle. Listen to your pastor. Listen to your Bible teachers, your elders, your deacons. Pay attention to them. If you are in a Bible-believing church, what the leaders have to say will reveal truth to you.

Proverbs 4:20 says, "*My son, attend to my words, incline thine ear unto my sayings. Let them not depart from thine eyes; keep them in the midst of thine heart. For they are life* [shout life!] *unto those that find them, and health to all their flesh.*"

Isn't that exciting? All the life and health you need is right here in this Bible.

2. We must love the truth. I believe if you truly know the truth, you are going to love the truth.

"And then shall that Wicked be revealed, whom the Lord shall consume with the spirit of his mouth, and shall destroy with the brightness of his coming: Even him, whose coming is after the working of Satan with all power and signs and lying wonders, And with all deceivableness of unrighteousness in them that perish; because they received not the love of the

truth, that they might be saved. And for this cause God shall send them strong delusion, that they should believe a lie: That they all might be damned who believed not the truth, but had pleasure in unrighteousness." (2 Thessalonians 2:8-12)

These verses teach us that because people did not receive a love of the truth that God allowed them to be deceived, deluded and to believe a lie, because they didn't love the truth when they heard it.

I love my wife. Forty years I've been married to her, and it's amazing, she still stays with me. She's a gift from God. She's my wife and I love her. So every now and again, I embrace her. You know whatever you love you're going to embrace. You're going to grab hold of it. You're going to pull it to you.

If you love the truth, you're going to grab hold of it. You're going to embrace it. You are going to pull it to you. You won't let it just go in one ear and out the other. You won't just allow it go by. When you hear the truth, and you love the truth, you will embrace the truth.

This is how we're going to win the battle for truth in our society. We have an entire generation of young people that have been deceived and are blinded to the truth. Because in many of our colleges and universities and schools, the truth has been removed from them. In some local school districts or educational systems, teachers have been allowed more freedom to talk about Jesus, creation, a Godly worldview, and responsibility to God. That freedom is continually being challenged to the point that in many districts, teachers are not allowed to have a Bible on their desk or even wear a cross around their neck.

At the university level, students have been threatened with failing grades and refusal to graduate if they mention any biblical principles, creation, or anything that doesn't line up with the philosophy of that university. Because of the impact universities and the media have, Jesus has increasingly become a "No-No" in our society.

You're going to have to know what you believe. You're going to have to love it enough to do the next thing here to win the battle for truth, you must defend the truth.

3. We must defend the truth. We've discussed the fact that you have to know the truth, and that you have to love the truth of the Word of God. But now you have be prepared to defend the truth.

"Beloved, when I give all diligence to write unto you of the common salvation, it is needful for me to write unto you, and

exhort you that ye should earnestly contend for the faith which was once delivered unto the saints." (Jude 3)

We are to assert a position of faith and strive in opposition against any position that seeks to dispute the truth of God's Word. We are to vie for the faith that was once delivered to the saints. You have to contend for it. You must stand up for it. We must defend the truth of God's Word. You and I are the only ones that can do it. And I have news for you...we must do it together in the wisdom of God. We must have the wisdom of God to get His strategy regarding what to do and what to say. Timing is a key element in strategy. God may have you, like Daniel, learn the Babylonian system, but also remain true to your God. Being there outside of a class or after work for the other students or co-workers to discuss "truth" could be God's strategy for reaching people who have honest questions. Many have been brought to "the truth" when they hear irrational statements made by teachers or professors, and seek out someone else in the class who may know "the truth."

"Only let your conduct be worthy of the gospel of Christ, so that whether I come and see you or am absent, I may hear of your affairs, that you **stand fast in one spirit, with one mind striving together for the faith of the gospel."** (Philippians 1:27 NKJV - emphasis mine)

Get into reforming the laws of our society. Get involved with politics. Get out there and help win the battle. We need people who will do that. Thank God for the National Rifle Association nowadays. These guys are fighting for the truth, our Second Amendment rights. They're defending the truth. We need some warriors. We need some people who are going to fight for the truth.

This is our Christian responsibility because we are the pillar and ground of truth. The Bible said that we have the truth. If we don't do it, who will do it? The whole world will go to darkness. You are the light of the world, I am the light of the world. Jesus said to work while it's day. *"I must work the works of him that sent me, while it is day: the night cometh, when no man can work. As long as I am in the world, I am the light of the world."* (John 9:4-5)

That is the key there....while you are in this world, you are the light of the world. Because one of these days your light is going to go out. You are going to leave this world. The Bible says, "While it's day we work." What makes daytime the time to work? Because there is light. When the light goes out it's nighttime. No man can work when it's nighttime, the Bible says.

As long as you are in the world and I am in the world, it's light right now. It's daytime. We have to work to defend the gospel of Jesus Christ. I am excited when I get the opportunity to resist the falsehoods surrounding Jesus, which gives me an open door to speak the truth of the Word of God. I fight to keep the truth of the Gospel from being taken away for the unbeliever. It's not my desire that any would perish, so I work hard to keep that truth in the earth by speaking and writing in support of the doctrines of Jesus.

I don't know about you, but while I'm alive, I will be working. I will avail myself to His Word (truth). I am going to love the Word (truth). And I am going to defend the Word (truth) that will free men from their sin. We were made to defend the truth of the Word of God. This is our Christian responsibility.

"Sanctify them through thy truth: thy word is truth." (John 17:17)

4. We must speak the truth. *"But speaking the truth in love, may grow up into him in all things, which is the head, even Christ."* (Ephesians 4:15)

We must speak the truth. There is such a spirit of intimidation against us as Christians in the world today. People say that we are intolerant because we come out and say that there is such a thing as moral absolutes.

The biggest thing that caused the Roman government and the religious people to be against Jesus and to crucify Him was because He said that there were moral absolutes.

Moral Absolutism is defined as the ethical belief that there are absolute standards against which moral questions can be judged, and that certain actions are right or wrong, regardless of the context of the act.

Jesus makes a statement in John 14:6 that sends the whole earth in a tailspin. *"I am the way, the truth, and the life: no man cometh unto the Father but by me."* Since Jesus is the way, it makes all other ways obsolete and without relevance. In other words, "...there is only one way to get to the Father, and that way is narrow and without options. It's a singular pursuit."

Today, we have religious pluralism and diversity. When you stand up and say that there is only one way to God, people say, "No, that's intolerance of everybody else's belief." That's when we must remember that we are here on earth to defend or contend for the faith. We are not going to be loved in this world. Jesus has already told us that we are going to be, *"...hated by all men for my sake."* (Matthew 10:22)

The current presentation in defense of this type of thinking is that there is truth in every religion. There is a little truth in every religion. But know this, Jesus didn't say that He was **some** truth. He didn't say that He was **made up** of truth. He didn't indicate on any level that He was a **piece** of this and a **part** of that. No, He was very clear..."I am **THE** Truth."

The word, 'the' is absolute, singular, directive to the final of a subject. Jesus is 'the' truth. In other words, truth starts and ends with Jesus.

The trouble in our society is that it has tolerated everything under the sun, and even though many leaders know that this depraved thinking has gone too far, they lack the ability to speak the truth. But you and I have not only a responsibility but a command from God himself to speak the truth, albeit in love.

You have to know that when you take a stand that doesn't agree with the prevailing motto: "If it works for them, who are you to say, that it's not right?" When you stand up and say, "That's not the way. There is only one way," you are going to be labeled a religious bigot. It will be said that you are intolerant and you don't have love for others. The reality is that my love for others is what motivates me to give them the truth.

Like I said, there is great intimidation against God's people to speak the truth today. When you stand up for a moral absolute in a world of relativism, where they say there are no absolutes, then you become a person that is looked at as a problem. For example, at your job, if you say that marriage should be between one man and one woman, then you become known as a religious hate-monger.

We cannot run from it. We cannot hide from it. We are in a battle for truth. It's a battle and it's a battle that we can win! God is on our side, Hallelujah!

"What shall we then say to these things? If God be for us, who can be against us?" (Romans 8:31)

We can win this battle. But we must be in the fight. You can't win a battle that you're not in.

Chapter 5

THE BATTLE FOR THE FAMILY

"After this manner therefore pray ye: Our Father which art in heaven, Hallowed be thy name. Thy kingdom come, Thy will be done in earth, as it is in heaven. Give us this day our daily bread. And forgive us our debts, as we forgive our debtors. And lead us not into temptation, but deliver us from evil: For thine is the kingdom, and the power, and the glory, forever. Amen." (Matthew 6: 9-13)

God is a family Man. It was the very heart of a Father that caused God to begin the process of creation. God ultimately has the love of family at the center of His heart at all times. You see the nucleus of family throughout every page of the Bible. But now, more than ever, the heart of God is being tested, and His family dynamic is under attack.

Satan hates the family, because of what it represents. He was at one time part of the heavenly family, but now he will never have that love and support from God again. Yet we, as God's earthly creation through Jesus, have the love, support, and fellowship that is lacking in the dead realm, where he resides.

We also see the principles of the kingdom of God most demonstrated in family, and that's another reason why satan hates it so much.

The foundation of the family is God the Father. Then he created the man directly under Him as the next part of the family dynamic. I know if we look at society that it doesn't look as though the man (male) was created directly under God in the family dynamic, but the truth is we cannot win the battle for the family without the men.

I understand that things in the earth seem pretty messed up and even in your respective communities, men are absent and their presence is missed. But know that there are men who are picking up the torch and engaging the enemy for the family. Because every other battle will depend on us winning the battle for our families.

Women cannot win the battle for the family in our society today. No matter how things appear, they (women) can't do it. Why? Because the Bible says that the husband is the head of the wife. Ephesians 5 tells us that God has put man in the position of leadership in the home. However, this doesn't mean that the man is superior to the woman, because he isn't.

*"So God created man in his own image, in the image of God created he him; male and female created he **them**. And God blessed **them**, and God said unto **them**, Be fruitful, and multiply, and replenish the earth, and subdue it: and have dominion..."* (Genesis 1:27-28).

God created them as equals. In Christ you're equals. There is no superiority between men and women. But the fact is that God gave responsibility in the home to the man that He didn't give to the woman. He chose to do that not because man was superior, but that was God's choice.

Husband, be the head of the home. Husband, be the head of the wife. Well, what does that mean? How can I lead my family? As a man, how can I win the battle for the family?

Men are called to lead the family. How do we lead the family? I want to say this again, only the Christian man can restore the Biblical family. The women can't do it without the men, as hard as they try. We have to win the battle for the Christian home, because our society is collapsing. The family has been under attack, because men have been taken out of their position, either willfully or forcefully, and now our homes are in disarray.

Modern culture has feminized men today. Very few men out there today even knows what it means to be a man in the Biblical sense of the word. Guys, we can't win the battle for the family unless we take responsibility for our part, and it starts by getting back in a position of leadership. Here are three basic aspects to leading your family and thereby winning the battle:

1. You lead your family by loving your wife.

This is a big revelation to many, but it is a very important first step towards winning the battle for the family.

The Bible says, "*Husbands love your wife as Christ loved the Church*" (Ephesians 5:25). Did you know that God gave you your wife to teach you how to love like Jesus loves? Have you ever thought about that?

Husbands, love your wife as Christ loved the Church. What men need to understand is that nowhere in the Bible does God tell the woman that she has to love the man. And do you know why? Because she doesn't have to be told to love.

The Bible says that *"he that finds a wife finds a good thing and obtains favor from the Lord"* (Proverbs 18:22 NKJV). Well, what does that mean? What is the favor that you and I obtain from our wife? It is the love that she gives you that you don't deserve.

In other words, a woman has a gift to love a man. She is going to love him even when he's being a knothead. Listen men, I have to say these same things to myself, because I'm a man, too.

I had to learn this before I could tell it to you. God is trying to make us (men) Christ-like. Man had to be told to love his wife because he is naturally selfish. Leaders can be very selfish in making decisions. Love, however, sacrifices and doesn't want its own way, but rather what's best for the ones loved. Man had to be instructed because he doesn't have the innate gifting to love without instruction. God didn't leave anything to chance, He also told the man how to love his wife. *"...like Christ loved the Church and gave himself for her"* (Ephesians 5:25). We are supposed to love and cherish our wives. The man is also instructed to not be bitter against his wife, because he would naturally be bitter when she nags him, knows that answer before he does, or is insistent on her own way being right. So God commands the man to love and the Comforter shows him how to do it. The Father gives the grace and the Spirit shows the way, because no man understands his wife completely. It takes prayer and loving and listening in order to love his wife.

Fast forward to the problems that we're having today. Men have not kept their end of the deal. Men keep going to the bank and making withdrawals, as the wife keeps loving, even though she is not being nourished or cherished. And because of that we will keep going to the bank, making withdrawals without any intent of making a deposit. But a woman will keep giving, because that's how she was made, even when she is not being loved the way Christ loved the Church.

2. You lead your family by understanding your wife.

"Husbands, dwell with your wives according to knowledge as unto the weaker vessel, as heirs together in the grace of life, lest your prayers be hindered." (1 Peter 3:7)

Husbands have the responsibility to dwell with their wives according to knowledge. That means it's my job to understand my wife and her needs. God has commanded the wife to submit to and respect her husband's leadership. It is not natural for a woman to submit to her husband, but it is natural for her to love him. God created her to love and sacrifice, and the wife will normally sacrifice for the husband's career and for her family. However, it is natural for her to think that she knows what is best and to exert her own way, including withholding sex or affection.

It says, *"Husbands dwell with your wives as unto the weaker vessel."* We've taken that to mean that we are superior, because she's just a weak vessel. But what that really means is that she has different strengths and limitations. It is more natural for the wives to love their husbands as that is how God created them. If they are abused and mistreated until they no longer respect them, then they will quit loving, and leave, their husbands. What a woman doesn't respect, she won't follow. The warning signs are there, and if the man doesn't take heed, she will be gone. We have to understand what her limitations are. Because here's what happens: wives have a gift to love their husbands, but what happens is they love beyond their limits. No wife wants to see her husband fail.

That man isn't paying attention that that woman is just a shell now. Emotionally, she's just gone. She has not been nourished or cherished, she's just worn out. She just keeps loving by an act of her will, because she hasn't been loved and cherished and nurtured by her husband. Put value upon her. Affirm her. Make her feel like she is the Queen of the world.

Men, we have to win the battle for the family!

God is saying that He is coming home. He is rearranging things in your house, because He needs us to win the battle for the family and He knows that we cannot do it alone.

I have been an acting pastor for thirty-six years and have literally counseled thousands of couples. I know what I'm talking about. I am an expert in my business just like you are an expert in yours. If you do something for thirty-six years and you're not an expert, then you are just a dum-dum. You should be doing something else by now.

Sooner or later, you may lose that woman, if you don't understand your wife's weaknesses, her limitations, and you don't understand that she has been giving without receiving for too long now. If it's taken a toll on her, she may not leave you, but she'll be gone nonetheless. You can come to the bank one day and the account will be empty. She may say, "I love you but I gotta go. I love you, but I just can't live with you anymore."

Why? Because what you did was leave her an empty shell by taking all there was and never putting anything back in to replace what you withdrew.

And that is what's happened in our society. That's one reason why people have rejected Biblical marriage. That's one reason why people say that this

Biblical family thing just doesn't work. We should just live together; forget the commitment aspect of it. We don't need to sign papers, we just need to co-habitate. We need same-sex marriage, women are going to women to get the affection that they didn't get from the man.

They've given up on men. They say "men are so self-centered and selfish that they just bleed your dry; they just let you keep loving them and they won't give you anything back." This is happening and it's happening in the church. Because 50% of the people getting married today that are Christians are getting married for the second and third time.

And now we have Christian dating and Christian mingles all on television, which is all about getting online and finding your mate. I'm not saying that that's wrong at all. But what I am saying is that the family has broken down because the man has been "out to lunch."

Man has not been out there doing his job. Man has not been out there leading his home by loving his wife as Christ loved the Church and by understanding his wife.

I have to say this, please don't get mad at me guys, but somebody has got to say it. Because it has got to be said: so many of us men are still just boys.

Ladies, you need to know who you're marrying. You need to listen to your spiritual leadership before you come dragging this guy in saying that you are in love.

You need to check him out. You need to see where his maturity level is emotionally. Men, it's time to grow up. We grow up by taking responsibility. You can have all the faith in the world and still be immature. Faith doesn't mean you're mature. Faith comes by hearing the Word of God, but not maturity of character. You can hear the Word of God, understand it, and have faith, but it's obedience that makes you grow up.

That's why the Bible says, "*Children obey your parents in the Lord*" (Ephesians 6:1). Because you are not going to mature if you don't. Obedience is what makes people mature.

We've got to have help. We've got to save the family and it's all on the men.

To win the battle for the family, you must also:

3. Train your children in the things of God.

Ephesians 6:4 (NKJV) says, "*And you, fathers, do not provoke your children to wrath, but bring them up in the training and admonition of the Lord.*"

The instruction to the father is that he is the one that should be training his children in the things of God. But most of the time, men will let the Mom do that, because a lot of the guys don't even read their Bible.

Mom does her devotions faithfully, which is why children are dysfunctional. Dad is not there, or he's there but he's not functioning as a Biblical father in the home. Children should see Dad sitting down with his Bible. Your children should hear you praying. They should hear you saying, "We're going to church today!"

Instead, we have Mom getting up and getting the kids and herself ready for church. Then when she asks Dad if he's going, his response is more along the lines of "It's a beautiful day out today, I think that I'll go in the woods and meditate with the Lord." What a crock.

What he is really saying is, "I don't want to take responsibility for being the spiritual head of my children, so I'll evade my responsibility and sit back and let you do it." Men are running from their responsibility as spiritual leaders in the home.

A well-published study revealed that if the fathers went to church as an adult, their children were very likely to follow in their footsteps and attend as adults as well. However, if the father didn't attend church, his children were very likely to not attend as adults either. The study showed that the mother's influence on the children to attend church as an adult was significantly less than the father's influence. Men, we have to set the example, as our children are more likely to follow our example. God made it that way. When fathers get saved and go to church, most of the time they will bring their entire family to church.

The churches are full of programs and the men still aren't discipled, trained, or mentored. Ministry to men can be like herding cats - it is tough work. Men ask hard questions and put up with nonsense. They expect you to honor their time, because they are stretched. But if it adds value, gives them a feeling of worth, and helps them to be better men or fathers or husbands, they will be there. Pastors, you need to disciple and train your men. Most men have never been trained. Train your men how to pray, train them how to study and understand their Bible. Train them in Biblical patterns and principles. Get men involved in a men's ministry in your church and they will bring strength to your church. Young men and women will have godly influence from men in the church.

When a man feels comfortable and needed, he will be there. If he feels uncomfortable or doesn't feel like he is needed, he will stay away. If he sees disorganization and a lot of women, he is "out of there." Many churches are really designed for women and so the man is uncomfortable. The father and husband begin to see the church in competition with his God-given role. He sees the pastor in competition with his headship.

Seriously, pastors, the root cause that men aren't "spiritual" is that the men have not been discipled. Pastor, that is your job. Once the men are trained and discipled, they will handle the issues at home and your counseling load will go down. They just have never been trained. Once the men are trained to study and understand their Bibles, pray, lead devotions, take the lead in a godly way, they they will do all of the above. When a man doesn't know what to do and doesn't want to be embarrassed, he does nothing.

Many churches are designed so that men aren't necessary; the pastor does it all, so the man brings his kids to church, and if they go bad, he blames the church and the pastor. Pastor, establish a men's ministry where the men are given tools to succeed as a man on the job, in the community, and at home. There are several ministries out there to help you. And here is one of the important things men will learn:

"Fathers, provoke not your children to anger, lest they be discouraged." (Colossians 3:21)

Rules without relationship breeds rebellion. You cannot just take the position, "Do what I say because I said so." It's an antiquated way to develop your children.

That's how I was raised. It is the relationship that I had with my parents. There was no love and affection, and by the time I was 17-18 years old, you better believe that there was a whole lot of rebellion going on. Why? Because my parents looked at my sisters and brothers and me as a commodity to serve their needs. So my Dad would give me orders and not talk to me and that is what many of you are doing today.

If you develop a relationship with your children, fathers, they will want to obey you. Giving orders without relationship then demanding obedience is how you provoke your children to wrath. And the Bible teaches against it, because God is our Father and He doesn't function that way with us.

When we first come to God, all of our prayers are answered almost instantly. Everything is wonderful...God is so good. Then we enter the stage of our growth where, "*To whom much is given, much is required*" (Luke 12:48), and He asks us to do something for Him.

When God does this you have the attitude of "Why wouldn't I want to do this for Him, when He is so good and has done so much for me?".

Do you see what happened here? God doesn't start out with us making demands of us. He is completely interested and vested in building a solid relationship and displaying His love for us. Then He will start to place more responsibility on us, once we have grown a bit and can handle the pressure of those demands. Because at all times, He is more concerned about the relationship than anything else.

He is a good Father, our perfect example, and He is looking to develop great fathers after Himself. We are not going to win the battle for the family if we don't start taking our role and place in the family seriously. You and I are fighting for our grandchildren, who ten to fifteen years from now will be suffering in society if we don't step up right now and do something about it.

We have no choice; it's time to fight for our families and it starts with the men.

"And David smote them from the twilight even unto the evening of the next day: and there escaped not a man of them, save four hundred young men, which rode upon camels, and fled. And David recovered all that the Amalekites had carried

away: and David rescued his two wives." (1 Samuel 30:17-18)

When the Amalekites took the families of David and his men, David and part of his army went after the Amalekites and recovered all, including wives, children and goods. This is what it means to battle for your family, men.

We should be weeping before God about the condition that we find our world in today. But after we weep, we must put on out battle gear and engage the enemy, winning the battle for our wives, our children, and our substance by which we take care of them.

It's time to fight and win the battle for our families now more than ever.

Chapter 6

THE BATTLE FOR YOUR SOUL

"Dearly beloved, I beseech you as strangers and pilgrims, abstain from fleshly lusts, which war against the soul." (1 Peter 2:11)

What is your soul?

Just like your spirit, the soul is made up of three parts: the mind, will and emotions. Where does the battle for your soul start? In your mind.

Mind: controls what you think about

Will: influences the choices you make

Emotions: determine how you will feel

Before you got saved, you had a sinful nature. It has little to do with what your actions. A newborn baby has a sinful nature. We know this because the Bible tells us that we were all *"born in sin and shaped in iniquity"* (Psalm 51:5). That has nothing to do with you, this comes straight down the bloodline from Adam and Eve and a piece of fruit in a garden.

But when that happened, your birth ensured that you would without hesitation be drawn to sinful, unlawful acts like a moth to a flame. And as you grew, you experimented and tasted sin and all that it offers. Your members (body) were used to fulfill every desire of your soul.

Sin is a spiritual thing, something that can never be underestimated, nor its propensities overlooked. Before you got saved, your body was a slave to sin as it (sin) sought to gratify itself. In the process, your body developed certain appetites (lusts of the flesh) for things that are unlawful.

Now that you are born-again, your spirit was recreated spiritually. Hear me, your spirit was made new, **not** your soul. Your soul still had to be saved. It wasn't at the time that you made the decision for Christ.

"Wherefore lay apart all filthiness and superfluity of naughtiness, and receive with meekness the engrafted word, which is able to save your souls." (James 1:21)

Sin is the nature of satan and is demonic in every way. Like I said, your spirit has been recreated, but now your soul has to be restored (saved).

Now that you have God's life in you, the Holy Spirit wants to use your body, your members, for God's desires and His purposes. That is where the battle is waged. The body (the Bible calls it your flesh) still wants what it was getting through gratification. The new-born spirit now wants to gratify the desires and purposes of God. World War III has ensued in the spirit because of this very powerful divide.

The fleshly lusts are waging war against your soul. Those desires are getting into your mind. They will try to get in and dominate your thought life until you surrender. All you can find yourself doing is thinking about that unlawful thing that your body wants.

What many people underestimate and many churches fail to teach is that when you get saved, your body that was trained by sinful, unlawful acts often times still craves and wants those things after your conversion experience.

It is so important to teach this so that people don't think that their salvation 'didn't take' because they are still having those desires and feelings that they know are sinful.

Take for example someone who was a heavy drinker before they got saved. They have given their life to Christ and they stopped drinking. Then one day all of a sudden, they think about a drink. If they don't immediately take that thought captive, they will continue to think about a drink, until they can start to 'feel' how that drink would taste going down their throat. Pretty soon, they will start to 'feel' the drink in their hand and before you know it, they will have a full commercial running in their head about taking a drink.

When that happens, you will find them pulling up to the nearest liquor or wine store to satisfy what the flesh told them that they wanted. And all of it started with a thought.

The same is true of any unlawful act that plays out in your life. It starts with a thought, every single time!

"Casting down imaginations, and every high thing that exalteth itself against the knowledge of God, and bringing into captivity every thought to the obedience of Christ." (2 Corinthians 10:5)

Alright, now let's go back and deal with the mind. When something gets in your mind and you think about it long enough, it creates an emotion. And because thoughts create feelings, before you know it you are actually living out in your heart the experience you started in your head.

You will start 'feeling it' which moves you right on into 'doing it'. Let me tell you, it is not a far leap at all. That is why you have to be diligent in guarding your thought life.

When your mind, your will and your emotions are unguarded, you will lose the battle for your soul. It is just that simple. But make no mistake; it starts with your thought life. That engendered thought, desire, passion, moved to an emotion that ultimately resulted in a choice that sped into an action.

Don't let the movie play in your head. If I can tell you anything about winning the battle of your soul, it would be without hesitation, guard your thought life. Become a good steward over your thought life. You have the power to do just that, because if you don't, you will end up panting like a dog after things that God says you should have no part of.

That is exactly how believers end up needing deliverance from things because they have let their thought life run wild, acting out everything that comes to their mind. Which is how you let demons get in your head and your soul. They take hold in there and you get to a point where you can't even help yourself anymore. It's not even you anymore. You want to quit but you can't because you're demonized. You need deliverance, by having the devil cast out of you.

The devil is not playing with you and this isn't a game. You win the battle for your soul by protecting your thought life. Because if you don't pretty soon you'll have seven more demons more wicked than the one before him.

Then you will have entered into a place where you are going to need a lot of help. Plus, demons bring sickness, disease, poverty, confusion, and a bunch of other things with them. Believe me, they don't come empty-handed. They come with every vile thing that they are made of, with one goal: to carry out the mission of *"killing, stealing, and destroying."* (John 10:10)

Always remember that the goal of a thought is to graduate into an action. The same is true for business owners and inventors. Every company, business endeavor, book, scientific discovery, health cure, etc. - every single one of them started as a thought.

Thoughts in and of themselves are not bad. The thought becomes dangerous when it reveals the type of negative, ungodly information that it is carrying to your mind. And that is where we need to grow in selecting and filtering thoughts that don't align with God's Word.

"Finally, brethren, whatsoever things are true, whatsoever things are honest, whatsoever things are just, whatsoever things are pure, whatsoever things are lovely, whatsoever things are of good report; if there be any virtue, and if there be any praise, think on these things." (Philippians 4:8)

You see from the verse above that there are thoughts that are just, pure, lovely and are of a good report. God says, "I'm not telling you not to think, just think on these kinds of things." Why would He say that? Remember what I said before. A thought is ultimately trying to graduate out of your mind into the world through your actions. And you cannot allow those negative, unlawful, sinful thoughts a graduation day.

There is a quote that I like that says, "You can't stop birds from flying over your head, but you can stop them from making a nest in your hair." You can't stop thoughts from coming. Thoughts will come, but you have the choice to determine which ones stay and for how long.

That's what it means to lose the war for your soul. But thanks be unto God that we can win the war for the soul. We have dominion over everything in the earth and that includes our thoughts. Our soul can prosper over our thought life!

"Beloved, I pray that you may prosper in all things and be in health, just as your soul prospers." (3 John 2 NKJV)

Chapter 7

THE BATTLE FOR THE FAITH

"Fight the good fight of faith, lay hold on eternal life, to which you were also called and have confessed the good confession in the presence of many witnesses." (1 Timothy 6:12 NKJV)

The battle for your faith is a big one. In this verse of scripture, we see a general talking to a spiritual son about warfare. And one of the things I've realized over the years is that people love the father (parent) aspect of the apostleship but not so much the general side of it. It's understandable because we all want to be nurtured and comforted and cared for. But there are times that the general side is necessary and is just as important as the parental side of the office. More than anything, we have to learn that parents raise up sons and daughters. But generals prepare soldiers who are ready to fight.

In this book, I'm in my generalship. I'm attacking the enemies of God. And I need to develop soldiers for that. So I'm not in my father mode. And as you mature you have to learn how to receive both, although you might prefer one side over the other. Because the battle for your faith is a crucial battle that you must win.

Satan is there to get you out of faith. So the real thing to know here is that the warfare is to stay in faith at all times. No matter what you are standing in faith for, don't allow the enemy to short-circuit you. You're better than that. You have got to stand no matter what you see, feel, taste, touch, or smell. Your five senses cannot dictate what you believe or how you believe.

What is faith?

Faith means that you know you have it and you don't have to see it, touch it, taste, it, smell it, or hear it to know that it exists. Many of you that have read my other materials have heard me talk about a sixth sense. As a believer you have another way of determining whether something is real or not - it's by your faith. Faith is another sense that tells you whether something actually exists. This is how you live.

You live knowing that you have something that your five physical senses have not perceived or discerned yet. So when you pray and believe God for an answer, you believe you have it, even though you haven't perceived it in the five sense realm yet. That's faith!

Staying right there in your heart, believing that you already have whatever it is, even though you can't feel it or smell it yet, you must keep believing that you have that job, that raise, that new business idea, that healing, whatever it is. You must keep believing by faith at all times. I have faith that you can win this battle.

"Verily, verily, I say unto you, He that heareth my word, and believeth on him that sent me, hath everlasting life, and shall not come into condemnation; but is passed from death unto life." (John 5:24)

Do you see that? He that believes has!

That is astounding! All you and I have to do is believe. Do the same thing you did to get saved, believe God's word (promise) to you. Believing is the possessing of a thing. You possessed your salvation by believing on the Lord Jesus Christ. Faith is like a hand that takes, which means you are not in faith until you can say, "I have it," and mean it.

The reason why most people have not seen the manifestations of their prayers is because they are waiting to see it, touch it, taste, hear it, or smell it, before they say that they have it. Those people have not gotten to faith yet. The only time you are in faith is when you can say that you have something that your five senses doesn't perceive yet.

Can you see now why satan would fight you over your faith? Let me give you this news though - he can't do a thing with it. Your faith was given to you in a measure, and he has no power to take it from you. I can also tell you that the more you use your faith, the stronger and more powerful it will become. It's like exercising muscles; the more you believe God, the more you will be able to believe Him.

Again, that is where the fight of faith resides: satan will do everything he can to get you to look at the sense realm as your confirmation of what you have or don't have. He is going to try and back you in a corner and make you produce some tangible evidence that you have what you say you have. And guess what, you have all the evidence you need.

*"Now **faith is** the assurance (**the confirmation, the title deed**) of the things [we] hope for, being **the proof** of things [we] do not see and the conviction of their reality [faith perceiving as **real fact** what is not revealed to the senses]."* (Hebrews 11:1 AMP)

Your faith is your tangible evidence! Hallelujah! So when satan comes and asks you to produce ownership papers, just pull out your faith, it's the title deed (deed of ownership).

For example, if I go online and purchase a car and the company or person sends me the title to the car. Do I own the car, even though it hasn't been delivered to my house yet?

Yes. I own the car and I can prove it by the deed I hold in my hand.

The same is true for what you are believing for. Your faith means you own something although it hasn't been delivered to your house yet. The law says, when you have the title deed, then you've got whatever it's the title to.

Don't let your five senses talk you out of your deed. It doesn't matter what it is. Unfortunately, the reason most people don't receive answers to their prayers is because of that right there. They let the physical realm dictate what they have in the spiritual realm. Then they get talked right out of faith over a feeling. Don't let that happen to you.

"Then touched he their eyes, saying, According to your faith be it unto you." (Matthew 9:29)

Jesus said things are manifested in your life according to your faith. Which means, do you have faith to start something and not finish? Do you have faith for two or three days and then you get like Peter?

Peter's faith got him out of a boat in the middle of a storm. His faith caused him to stand on water, but his faith couldn't hold him so he could make it to Jesus. Is that you? Does your faith get you so far and then it short-circuits at a certain point? Peter had faith that lasted him a little while, but then he started looking at the five senses and gave up.

Maybe I don't have it. Maybe I can't do this. Maybe, maybe, maybe. Next thing you know, we, like Peter, go down in faith and down in life. All because we couldn't hold on to faith when the wind (sense realm) starts to blow.

Don't let that be you...you can win the battle for your faith, you just have to believe.

The Bible says that Peter began to "look at the wind and waves" (representing the five sense realm), becoming fearful:

"But when he saw the wind boisterous, he was afraid; and beginning to sink, he cried, saying, Lord, save me. And immediately Jesus stretched forth his hand, and caught him,

and said unto him, O thou of little faith, wherefore didst thou doubt?" (Matthew 14:30-31)

Anytime we take our eyes off the Word of God and quit seeing through the eye of faith, we will be looking at the five sense realm that may tell us what we are believing is impossible and cannot happen.

"While we look not at the things which are seen, but at the things which are not seen: for the things which are seen are temporal; but the things which are not seen are eternal." (2 Corinthians 4:18)

That is when fear will take over and enter the heart, choking out our faith which was solely based upon the Word of God plus nothing, seeing the situation through the lenses of the Word of God. To illustrate how faith works, we should look to the "father of faith," which is Abraham, a man who "walked by faith and not by sight." Paul told the Romans that they should "follow the steps of Abraham's faith," and so should we as modern day believers.

"And the father of circumcision to them who are not of the circumcision only, but who also walk in the steps of that faith of our father Abraham, which he had being yet uncircumcised....(As it is written, I have made thee a father of many nations,) before him whom he believed, even God, who quickeneth the dead, and calleth those things which be not as though they were. Who against hope believed in hope,

that he might become the father of many nations, according to that which was spoken, So shall thy seed be. And being not weak in faith, he considered not his own body now dead, when he was about an hundred years old, neither yet the deadness of Sarah's womb: He staggered not at the promise of God through unbelief; but was strong in faith, giving glory to God; And being fully persuaded that, what he had promised, he was able also to perform." (Romans 4:12, 17-21)

What were the steps in his faith that produced the miracle enabling Abraham and Sarah to have a child at the ages of 75 and 100 years old? First of all, it says that Abraham *"believed according to that which was spoken."* His faith was based solely on what God had said to him, "so shall your seed be like the stars of heaven and the sand of the seashore." Just like us, to whom God has said, "By his stripes you were healed," we have to make the decision which we will believe, the Word of God or the five sense realm that may be contradictory. Abraham chose to believe that "he was the Father of many nations," even before there was any evidence in the natural realm to prove his belief. Next, he did "not consider his body (being old) and the deadness of Sarah's womb" as any reason for doubting the Word of God. Abraham refused to doubt what God had said based on his physical condition at the time. Faith is like that sixth sense we have as believers; the Bible calls it "believing with the heart."

"For with the heart man believeth unto righteousness; and with the mouth confession is made unto salvation." (Romans 10:10)

Instead of believing what the fives senses tell us, even thought it is very real, we should move from the sense realm into the faith realm by "believing with the heart" independently of the five senses. This is what it means to "walk by faith" because *"faith perceives as a real fact that which is not yet revealed to the five physical senses."* (Hebrews 11:1 AMP)

The next step that Abraham took toward his faith-wrought miracle was to "call those things which be not as though they were." Faith in the heart is always released through the words of our mouth, as Jesus said in Mark 11:23-24 (NKJV):

"For assuredly, I say to you, whoever says to this mountain, 'Be removed and be cast into the sea,' and does not doubt in his heart, but believes that those things he says will be done, he will have whatever he says. Therefore I say to you, whatever things you ask when you pray, believe that you receive them, and you will have them."

Abraham called himself by the new name God had given him. His name had previously been Abram, meaning "High Father," but when God gave him the promise of children He changed it to Abraham, meaning "Father of a multitude." Abraham believed "according to that which was spoken" and began to speak of himself accordingly. He changed his confession to agree with what God had spoken about him even before Sarah was pregnant with any sign of a child. Faith doesn't wait to see any physical evidence before making a confession of possession; it speaks solely on the basis of what God has said that has been revealed in the heart of an individual.

I have used this faith principle to receive from God time and again. Someone once said that when a person understands how faith works, they have received something greater than anything that faith can produce. Learning how to use our faith to receive from God for the needs of life is itself a greater blessing than getting the things we need for now we have the means to live in victory all the time no matter what the need may be. It's like the old saying, "You can give a hungry man a fish to feed him for a day, or you can teach him how to fish to feed him for life." Which is the greater blessing?

When I first started pastoring a church in 1980, I was leading the Praise and Worship with my guitar, and I am not particularly gifted in this area, although anointed. When I was on the platform by myself on Sunday mornings, I would frequently look out at the people and say, "How do you like our praise team, we have the best praise them in the city, don't they sound wonderful!" People would look at me like my elevator didn't go all the way up, but I was "calling those things which be not as thought they already were." Little by little the singers and musicians began to show up and join the team until we had the most talented praise team of any church in our city. When a nationally-known evangelist came to our city for a crusade, our praise team was called for the opening service.

Later on while in ministry, my heart began to give me problems as a result of the Rheumatic Fever I had as a child, and the drugs I used before coming to Christ. There were times that I would lose my vision while preaching, and could not walk up three steps without getting out of breath; I was dying while in my mid-thirties. God had graciously revealed the secrets of faith to me that I am sharing with you so that I could pray and believe that I had received a new heart, even while the symptoms where still raging in my body.

"Therefore I say to you, whatever things you ask when you pray, believe that you receive them, and you will have them." (Mark 11:24 NKJV)

I would continually say with my mouth out loud, "Lord, thank you that I have a new heart. I will live and not die and declare the works of the Lord." After some weeks of standing in faith, God dropped a new heart in my chest at age 35. I was healed without the aid of medical science or medications, and ran five miles on my fiftieth birthday, and six miles on sixtieth birthday. I am presently 65 years of age and plan to run seven miles on my seventieth birthday! The late and great evangelist R.W. Shambach used to say, "You don't have a problem, all you need is faith in God." I agree!

Chapter 8

THE BATTLE FOR YOUR MINISTRY

"This charge I commit unto thee, son Timothy, according to the prophecies which went before on thee, that thou by them mightest war a good warfare; Holding faith, and a good conscience; which some having put away concerning faith have made shipwreck: Of whom is Hymenaeus and Alexander; whom I have delivered unto Satan, that they may learn not to blaspheme." (1 Timothy 1:18-20)

Ministry means 'to serve'. It's that simple. People try to make it mean a bunch of other things, but it simply means service. With that said, would you say that everyone has a ministry of some kind? That God has a place for everyone to serve? The truth is that God has called all of us to ministry, because He has placed gifts in each one of us.

"For the gifts and calling of God are without repentance." (Romans 11:29)

So when you start asking yourself, "What should I be doing?", all you need to do is to start looking at your gift. Wherever your gift is, that's where your ministry is or where you area of service is located.

Every one of us has a ministry, a way to serve, and it's in our gifts. For instance, I am serving you as I write this book, because this is where one of my giftings lie. This is what I do.

There was at time when I didn't have this gift, so I would work in the nursery at church with the little ones. Then I moved to singles ministry. As I developed my gifts, I served in different areas. That's why people should be serving in their church. There is so much to do for the kingdom of God, every hand should be on deck for service.

In this scripture we have already discussed that Paul is talking to Timothy and calls him a 'true' son. This is a spiritual father trying to prevent shipwreck in one of his sons. He is sounding the alarm: "Timothy, the battle for your ministry is on!"

In order to win this battle for your ministry, Timothy, you are going to have to use the prophecies that I have spoken over you as your weapon. This warfare is going to be over your place of service and you can't forget those prophecies, because your ministry will depend on it.

Paul said, "Wage a good warfare with those prophecies Timothy!" Satan will battle with you over the prophetic words in your life. Don't be surprised when it happens, be prepared.

He will also war with you over the relationship that you have with your spiritual father by trying to make you doubt the validity of the prophetic word spoken over you by him. Don't allow him to come between that relationship. Guard it. Protect it, because it's precious and powerful.

"Keep the faith and a good conscience." (1Timothy 1:19)

In other words have a good conscience towards God and those He put in your life. Don't talk about the man of God behind his back, even if others do. Don't have a spirit of betrayal or Absalom on you. Don't say one thing and then do another. Have a good conscience by doing what's right when no one else is watching. That's how you sleep soundly at night.

If you don't, you can't have a clear conscience towards God and believe me, it will affect every other area of your life and you will shipwreck. He mentions two others who actually ended up shipwrecked and I believe since Paul saw what happened in his relationship with them, he wanted to prevent the same thing from happening with Timothy.

"...which some have rejected." (v. 19)

He mentions two of his other spiritual sons, Hymenaeus and Alexander. We know that they were spiritual sons because of how Paul handles them in the next verse. *"Whom I have delivered unto Satan, that they may learn not to blaspheme."* (v. 20)

Paul starts out telling Timothy how to fight the battle of his ministry and then ends talking about him turning two men over to satan so that they might learn a lesson. How did he make that leap?

Paul was explaining to Timothy that there is a price to pay; a reprimand ahead for those who don't do things God's way. To serve is a privilege, and that service/ministry is going to be tested and will become a place of battle at some point. Paul wanted to equip Timothy as any good father would, how to win victory in this area. Unfortunately, there are people who are forced to learn lessons the hard way, and this was one for two of his sons. Paul didn't want Timothy to become the third. He also knew that in order to really drive this point home about being of a good conscience, a few live examples would help.

So he references two of his fellow brothers under Paul's charge. Timothy knew these guys because Paul wouldn't bring up two men that Timothy didn't know to drive home a point. He tells Timothy very simply that I had to take my hands off of Hymenaeus and

Alexander because they didn't believe in what I was saying. They were not of a good conscience before God or myself. They didn't respect my position in their lives and didn't place value on what God has placed in me for their lives and ministry.

So I had to remove them from my covering. When that happens, they will be fair game for satan, and he will kill, steal and destroy to the point that they will be running back to the covering that they didn't appreciate in the beginning.

When you are in a battle for your ministry, your covering is paramount. God places spiritual fathers in the Body of Christ for a reason. He has given the five-fold ministry gifts for a reason. And when you don't respect those gifts to the body, you blaspheme not against the man, but against God.

We must always realize and be assured that it is satan who wants to steal our destiny and destroy our ministry effectiveness. When Peter was being tempted to betray Jesus as the Lord was being falsely accused and the stage was being set for His crucifixion and death, it was revealed to him that satan was behind his change of mind toward his leader.

"And the Lord said, 'Simon, Simon! Indeed, Satan has asked for you, that he may sift you as wheat. But I have prayed for

you, that your faith should not fail; and when you have returned to Me, strengthen your brethren." (Luke 22:31-32 NKJV)

Spiritual warfare against your ministry happens when the enemy suggests to your thinking such things as, "you cannot trust your leadership, they don't have your best interests at heart." Another "fiery dart" is "you are just being used and you will never get to do what God has called you to do." These and many others arrows of destruction are in satan's arsenal that he uses to separate proteges from their mentors and spiritual fathers. Of course all these weapons only have effectiveness where a person is more concerned about "self" than anything or anyone else. This is why Jesus told Peter to *"Deny yourself, take up your cross and follow me."* (Luke 9:23) When we are too "self-focused," we are more subject to be taken out by the enemy of our lives, and of God's Kingdom.

All successful servants of God came through a process of refinement for the call on their lives by being connected with a spiritual father and mentor in their lives. God has not changed his order for raising up champions of the faith, so instead of seeking our ministry, we should seek out the divine relationships that will propel us into our destiny. Scripture abounds with examples of these kinds of relationships.

Moses thought he should "jump into ministry" prematurely, and then found out that he needed forty years of training under his father-in-law Jethro before he was finally ready to be a "shepherd of Israel" (Exodus 18).

Elisha spent years as the servant of Elijah before being granted the Double Portion anointing that enabled him to be twice as productive as his spiritual father (1 Kings 19:19).

Saul served alongside a more mature man of God named Barnabas before being renamed Paul and thrust into apostleship to the Gentiles (Acts 13:1-4).

Timothy, the great apostolic leader of the Ephesian church, was the well-proven spiritual son of Paul (Philippians 2:19-23).

The Disciples became the "apostles of the Lamb" after three and a half years of mentorship under Jesus, who was serving as their apostle and spiritual father while on earth (Luke 22:28-29).

And so the pattern remains for all of us to follow. When many left Jesus after hearing some of the "hard sayings," *He asked his disciples, "Will you also go away?" They answered, "Lord, to whom shall we go? You have the words of eternal life."* (John 6:67-68)

There is a powerful relationship principle here in this passage that we cannot overlook and still progress in our calling. We must recognize those whom God is using to speak into our lives. Very often it is our spiritual parents that "have spiritual words" for us that have a profound impact on our lives. Sure, we can take advice and counsel for many mature believers, but they can never replace the persons that God has set in our lives to provide oversight and direction as we journey towards destiny. It is only the words of these God-appointed leaders that will bring activation and release into all that God has for us. This is why satan works night and day to try and separate us from these key people who have been anointed by God to serve our destiny. When Jesus told Peter that is was satan who had desired to have him, and sift him as wheat (meaning to separate like the wheat from the chaff), the Lord proceeded to tell him that the adequate intercession was made to secure victory for Peter and that he would recover himself and be restored to ministry on the Lord's side.

"But I have prayed for you, that your faith should not fail; and when you have returned to Me, strengthen your brethren." (Luke 22:32)

This ministry of revelation and intercession is the responsibility of our spiritual parents as they watch for our souls.

"Obey them that have the rule over you, and submit yourselves: for they watch for your souls, as they that must give account, that they may do it with joy, and not with grief: for that is unprofitable for you." (Hebrews 13:17)

You can win the battle for your ministry by staying connected to those God-ordained relationships. You will always know for sure who they are - satan will help with that by making the pressure to break away almost unbearable, so that we are tempted to bail out just for relief.

Remember the prophetic words spoken over your life, and who has spoken them; wage a good warfare and come out victorious as you are promoted into your calling.

None of these aforementioned battles can be won without a surrendered life to Jesus or submission to spiritual leadership and authority. Those two things are primary elements when it comes to winning the battles for truth, family, your soul, your faith, and your ministry.

Hopefully, you understand the gravity and intensity of the battles that you will be faced with if you haven't already. If not today, then one day you will have to engage in the battles that are before us as believers. I can tell you that you don't have to go looking for a fight - these battles will come find you, if you choose to sit at home with your hands in your lap. Because the moment you made Jesus the Lord of your life, you were enlisted in these battles. There is nothing you can do to avoid the fight. The only thing you can do now is get dressed.

Chapter 9

GETTING DRESSED FOR BATTLE

"Put on the whole armour of God, that ye may be able to stand against the wiles of the devil. For we wrestle not against flesh and blood, but against principalities, against powers, against the rulers of the darkness of this world, against spiritual wickedness in high places." (Ephesians 6:11-12)

All this talk about battle requires me to address one very important element of training, which is how to dress properly.

Of course I'm not talking about putting on a pair of pants or skirt. I'm talking about getting dressed for battle with an enemy that you can't see. That takes a different uniform all together.

When we prepare for war with our enemy, we must remember that although part of this battle is taking place on earth, its origin is in the spiritual realm, meaning we have to dress for a spiritual battle.

Ephesians 6:11-18 outlines what we need to be properly dressed for these battles:

Loins--Truth

Simply put, loins are the area of our bodies that deal with reproduction. We are to reproduce the truth of God's Word in our society in the dispensation in which we live.

Being dressed with truth is what will keep you steady during these battles. Yes, we have a ton of options when it comes to facts, but we don't function in the facts, we derive our guidance on a different realm.

"...thy word oh Lord is truth." (Psalm 119:160)

Knowing the Word of God will keep you adequately dressed for the fight. We see the effectiveness of knowing the Word of God and putting it to action in Matthew 4:4 - *"It is written..."* The only way to fight the enemy is with the Word of Truth, just like Jesus did.

Breastplate--Righteousness

The vital function of the breastplate in war is to protect the torso from injury. The torso is one of the most vulnerable areas of the body because so many major organs are located there.

"Righteousness exalts a nation..." (Proverbs 13:34)

Jesus secured our righteousness through His shed blood. We get to partake of His righteousness when come under His lordship. Part of our salvation is taking on the right-standing with the Father that was paid in the process of our new creation citizenship. God is not holding anything against us, because of the righteousness that Jesus secured for us.

You can go into battle with the peace of right-standing with God through any maneuver or tactic that the enemy tries to send your way. You are righteous in Christ. You don't have to hold your breath, wondering what God is thinking towards you.

The Bible announces that His thoughts towards us are good, not evil, to bring us to an expected end. (Jeremiah 29:11)

The accuser will work to take your eyes off of that truth. You are righteous. Don't let him steal that assurance from you. It can be just that weakness that he needs to attack you as your torso is unprotected.

Remember to put on your breastplate of righteousness.

Feet--Gospel of Peace

Have your feet covered with the good news of peace. What a powerful position! God is covering our feet so that as we walk through the valley of the shadow of death, (which is what these battles may feel like at times), we don't have to fear any evil thing. Not only is He with us, our feet or the vehicle of our movements are that of peace. Knowing that we can be at peace in the good news of the gospel, that God is at peace with us and therefore, we are at peace with Him.

Carrying that message to the world requires a steady foot, strong steps and a courageous balance. Our feet are to be covered, so that we aren't tripped up in battle. When peace is present there is comfort and clarity, no matter what confusion or violence is around us.

He gave us shoes for the battle, the gospel of peace.

Shield--Faith

Earlier in these pages we discussed faith as a battleground; a fight that you must win. But faith has another side to it. That same faith that you are battling over is also a shield about you.

Your faith will keep the arrows of fire from penetrating you, as you walk through diverse temptations.

"Count it all joy, my brothers, when you meet trials of various kinds, for you know that the testing of your faith produces steadfastness. And let steadfastness have its full effect, that you may be perfect and complete, lacking in nothing." (James 1:2-4 ESV)

Your faith is going to produce a steadfastness that is necessary for various trials (battles) that you might face. God is a shield about us and so He gives us faith as a weapon in these battles that we must win.

Head--Helmet of Salvation

I think the helmet of salvation is my favorite article of my uniform, because I understand that our minds can be a battlefield for the enemy's attack. When we accepted Jesus, salvation included the covering of the mind. You don't have to go crazy or have a nervous breakdown. God has provided for you a helmet that protects your mind from being taken by the demonic forces, if you will put your helmet on.

The helmet helps us to remember whose we are. That headpiece protects and helps bring to our remembrance the verses of scripture that need to be applied at different points in the fight.

Don't forget your helmet, because when the head is cut off the body has no choice but to follow. Just think about Goliath. David knew he had to cut off the head as a symbol that everything else about Goliath's stature was ineffective. If the enemy can cut off your head, he can take control of your body.

Whatever you do, don't forget your helmet.

Sword of the Spirit--The Word of God

I could write an entire book on this part of our battle armor, but I won't, at least not in this book. What I will say is that you must become like a skilled surgeon when it comes to the Word of God.

Of all the battle gear discussed, your sword is the only offensive component mentioned. The Bible refers to the Word of God as two-edged sword in two distinct places.

"For the word of God is living and active, sharper than any two-edged sword, piercing to the division of soul and of spirit, of joints and of marrow, and discerning the thoughts and intentions of the heart." (Hebrews 4:12 NKJV)

"In his right hand he held seven stars, from his mouth came a sharp two-edged sword, and his face was like the sun shining in full strength." (Revelation 1:16 NKJV)

Both of these verses tell us how sharp the sword of God really is. It can divide something that seems indivisible from a human standpoint. Who can divide the thoughts and intents of a person's heart, but God?

As John sees Jesus in Revelation, he sees a two-edged sword coming out of His mouth, which is the Word of God. Isn't it marvelous that we have been left with a weapon that is so precise that every battle and enemy can be subdued with the Sword of the Spirit? Only the Spirit of God can train and teach us how and when to maneuver such a powerful weapon!

Getting dressed for battle is a daily action that every believer must complete during our time of prayer and devotion to God. We must understand not only how crucial it is to be trained by our apostles and other leadership, but we must also take it upon ourselves to stand before God in prayer submission as we seek to be dressed daily for the battles that lie ahead of us.*

My prayer is that you will no longer sit on the sidelines while you act as a spectator in the battles raging on in our society and world. No longer can you, as a warrior in the faith, sit back comfortable and secure as long as your family is not affected. Because if one saint is battling, then we need all hands on deck until the enemies of God have been subdued and rendered helpless.

You have been enlisted, it's your time to get dressed and ready for your station. Whether you like it or not, you've been called to 'active duty' and you've got some battles to win!

*For my detailed teaching on the Armor of God, obtain the message "How to Be Strong in the Lord" from www.johnpolis.com.

ABOUT THE AUTHOR

Saved and spirit-filled in 1974, Dr. John Polis was called to ministry and graduated from Dayton Bible College with a BA in Biblical Studies in 1980, and a Master of Divinity from Florida Beacon College and Seminary in 1992. John was awarded the Honorary Doctor of Divinity from Florida Beacon in 1993 for his accomplishments in World Missions from 1983-93.

John and Rebecca, his wife of 42 years, have pastored for 36 years, planting churches in West Virginia and North and South Carolina. He is Founder and President of Revival Fellowship International, Inc., a Network of Churches and Ministers with affiliates in eleven states and six countries at the time of this writing. John also serves as an International Ambassador, and on the Advisory Council, for the International Coalition of Apostolic Leaders, and has conducted ministry on five continents, with books translated into Polish, Bulgarian, Croatian and Spanish. John and Rebecca have four children and six grandchildren.

BOOKS BY DR. JOHN POLIS

The Master Builder: Wisdom for Today's Apostles

Biblical Headship

The Kings Are Coming

Apostolic Advice

Recycled Believers - Solving the Mystery of Migrating Sheep

How To Produce Abundance in Your Life

Release The River Within You

Take My Yoke Upon You

Order these titles and more, as well as audio and video messages, at www.johnpolis.com. You can also follow Dr. John's blog at johnpolisblog.wordpress.com.